Bedside Stories

HOTELES

Bedside Stories

6

Hipólito G. Navarro

Andrés Neuman

Margarita Borrero

Guillermo Niño de Guzmán

nH
HOTELES

Published by ©NH Hoteles

Director of the collection: José Luis Martín Nogales

Cover design: NH Hoteles Marketing Department

Collection design and mock-up: José Luis Martín Nogales

Printed by Castuera

Translated by Bianca Southwood

Legal Deposit: NA 1656/2006

On the 27th April 2006, a jury made up of Espido Freire, José María Guelbenzu, Miguel Ángel Pérez Priego, Fernando Valls and José Luis Martín Nogales awarded the following NH Mario Vargas Llosa Prizes for Short Stories:

The Latest Mishaps, by Hipólito G. Navarro

Gengis Khan's Grave, by Francisco Javier Sánchez Serrano

Rules Are Rules, by Olga Merino

The short-listed stories were:

The Good Woman, by Margarita Borrero
Zoopathies, by Matías Candeira de Andrés
Road to Marseilles, by Abilio Estévez
Visitors' Book, by Andrés Neuman
The Kite, by Guillermo Niño de Guzmán

In the English category, a jury made up of María Teresa Gibert and José Antonio Gurpegui awarded the NH Mario Vargas Llosa Prize for Short Stories to:

Carrer Princesa, by Jamal Mahjoub

CONTENTS

HIPÓLITO G. NAVARRO, The Latest Mishaps 11

ANDRÉS NEUMAN, Visitors' Book 49

MARGARITA BORRERO, The Good Woman 67

GUILLERMO NIÑO DE GUZMÁN, The Kite 85

Hipólito G. Navarro

The Latest Mishaps

*H*ipólito G. Navarro *was born in Huelva in 1961 and currently lives in Seville. His novel* <u>Las medusas de Niza</u> *(The Jellyfish from Nice) was awarded the Ateneo Ciudad de Valladolid Prize and the Andalucía de la Crítica Prize in 2001. He worked as editor of the magazine* <u>Sin embargo</u>, *which focuses on story-writing. He has also had five collections of short stories published:* <u>El cielo está López</u> *(The Sky is López),* <u>Manías y melomanías mismamente</u> *(Mostly Manias and Melomanias),* <u>El aburrimiento</u> *(Boredom),* <u>Lester</u> *(Lester),* <u>Los tigres albinos</u> *(The Albino Tigers), and* <u>Los últimos percances</u> *(The Latest Mishaps).*

The writing of this author is non-conformist; he's always looking for new techniques, he likes to play with different registers, adding touches of humour, and is willing to risk exploring new literary methods. All of these characteristics are brought together in <u>Los últimos percances</u> *(Seix Barral), which has been awarded the NH Mario Vargas Llosa Prize for the best collection of short stories published in 2005.*

The Snow-Covered Head

As I leave the school, I sadly realize that yet another winter has come and gone without the snow settling on the ground, that there are only a few tiny flakes left spinning in the air, landing idly on the bare branches of the catalpa trees which line the road that goes up to the stand at The Roundabout. On the bend a bit further down, just by the Aroche Street junction I hear what sounds like the brakes of the Postie, the rickety old bus full of letters, so I set aside my meteorological melancholy and decide, without further ado, to make another bet: "I have to get to the Roundabout before he does, no running allowed". I have no way of knowing, however, that the old banger might be running late, nor do I suspect before making my bet that the driver is going to step quite so hard on the accelerator, which gives me such a fright that I have no choice but to quicken my pace if I really intend to get there first. Things start looking a bit tricky when I hear the driver lowering to second gear so he can make it even faster up the wet slope but there's not a lot I can do about it. These things happen. Then breaking one of my most sacred rules, I make a little sprint, a really short one, just enough to get a couple of metres ahead of the Postie, which rumbles into the Roundabout just as I am taking in a deep breath of frozen air. I have done it again, and this morning was an even bigger feat because my first appraisal of the weather was completely wrong and now the snow is falling heavily, crazily, twirling playfully before my eyes.

I have left the huge block of the school far behind, with its little trees slowly turning white, just like the dark green blackboards inside which will be covered with white chalk lines and scribbles by now. Somewhere between the school and my eyes, a bus manoeuvres and then stops and I see Emilio getting off it from the back door. Emilio works in the grain store on Benafique Street and as soon as I lay eyes on him I realize this would be a great chance to get even, as I am feeling uneasy after having cheated a bit before. I muck around for a while, knocking the icicles off the frozen surface of the fountain with my umbrella in order to give Emilio a bit of a head start, and when he reaches the big red gates of the bus depot, I make a new bet for myself, knowing just how hard it is going to be to get to the grain store before he does: the rascal is going flat out and I fear I have given him too much advantage.

Although I am naturally a bit absent-minded and snowflakes can unduly distract my attention, I reckon that I take between two and a half and three steps to each of Emilio's. But then taking into account that he has always been much taller than me and his legs cover more distance per step, I feel obliged to speed up a bit, yet not too much. I am more afraid of making the foolish mistake of running again than the possibility of slipping on the icy pavement and breaking a leg.

Meanwhile, although I have been trying to avoid it since I came out of her class, I succumb to thinking about Miss Esperanza, which has been happening for some months now. Her eyes, her slender, delicate hands, her wasp waist, her lips running through the letters, *m* and *a* spell *ma,* her suggestive perfume, her legs crossed under the table before so many innocent eyes submissively repeating *m* and *a* spell *ma,* thinking about all of her, in her entirety, until I realize that catching up with Emilio and overtaking him before he reaches the grain store is not going to be an easy feat, what with the snow which has started falling thickly and is settling dangerously under my feet.

My feet, once again, mechanically attempt to break into a trot, a wish I have no intention of letting them fulfil, because now I have got to thinking about Miss Esperanza, I want to dedicate my victory to her fair and square, without cheating.

Yet there are days when luck turns grey. Before my reckoning of how to get there before he does allows me to get too ecstatic over my imminent triumph, Emilio suddenly goes into Rosalía's bar, two hundred metres before reaching our set finishing line. So when I walk past the grain store, my victory seems hollow, senseless, and leaves me with a rather bitter aftertaste.

As I head back home, with the snow completely outwitting my umbrella by whirling up underneath it and soaking my face from every angle, I imagine myself appearing before Miss Esperanza empty-handed, without my trophy, my love-struck eyes looking secretly at her tiny chest as it rises and falls imperceptibly under her purple cardigan which I, in my dreams, tear off her with passionate kisses, undressing her completely and making her mine forever, *m* and *i* and *n* and *e* spell *mine,* mine, forever. I continue on my way, bumping into people, stopping from time to time to see if she is following me, and yet I know it will only ever be a dream, a fantasy, because the enormous age gap between us makes it all insane. Thirty? Thirty-five? Twenty, perhaps? I couldn't really care less. What are thirty years, after all? Ten thousand eight hundred days, I have it all worked out. But as far as she's concerned, ten thousand eight hundred days is an abyss filled with plans and if I take all the days and place them one after the other in a line, I could go around the world thirty-five times according to Jules Verne. I'm quite good at simple Mathematics and there are too many trips around the world in the abyss which separates us, Miss Esperanza.

I'm still going down the road, getting closer to home when I turn back once again and see Domingo in the distance with his three-wheeler van loaded with post bags, one last chance before I reach home to settle this whole business for once and for all. Now I have to reach the corner of the square before Domingo can overtake me in his jalopy. Now I am allowed to run, even though it looks like the snow is beginning to cover the ground and is becoming dangerous, but this time I have no choice, as there is no way this isn't going to happen unless Domingo's piece of junk falls to bits before catching up with me.

But I am just a boy. As hard as I try to grow up, I am still just a boy because I am fully aware of how dangerous it is, that I could easily fall over with the road being so wet and all... When I find myself on the ground the first thought that crosses my mind is Miss Esperanza, whether she has seen me fall, but luckily she is still at school. Most of all I am afraid that Domingo will beat me to the square so when two boys come and help me up I don't hang around or even thank them but rush off towards the corner, making it by a whisker, but before he does, I manage it, at last.

Finally, when I am almost home, I suppose I am not yet completely satisfied because when I see the clock on the tower is about to chime half past, I decide in a flash that I have to be inside sitting on the couch before I hear the bells. And indeed, when I sit down and look out the window at the snowflakes which seem to be getting bigger by the minute, it is not yet half past.

In the end I have beaten the Postie, Emilio, the young man from the grain store on Benafique Street, Domingo with his post bags and the bells. I smile slowly, the smile I know suits my face so well, just like the cigarettes I smoke on the sly in the bathroom because if anyone ever found out I smoke the odd cigarette all hell would break loose. Then, once I have rested a bit, I try to understand this need of mine to get to these finishing lines only I am aware of before anyone else can, but I give up. Psychoanalysis can come up with its own theories on sex and power and use me as a guinea pig for its own amusing experiments and deductions if it wants.

* * *

The truth is that my forecast about the last snowfall couldn't have been more mistaken because it snowed for two days and the town was almost cut off as a result. I had always liked heavy snowfalls up until a couple of months ago, but on this occasion the white postcard views I could see from my window grieved me deeply because the nursery has been closed since the first heavy snowfall and I have spent more days without seeing Miss Esperanza than my heart can bear. To make matters worse, the two days of snowfall were followed by one of those horrible long weekends with a bank holiday and then a holiday on the Tuesday for our patron saint. Almost a whole week without seeing her. What a distressing hiatus. So today, Wednesday, I am finally able to go back to the school and I am singing on the inside and fidgeting with the schoolbag I've prepared. The pencils, chalk pieces and rubbers all rattle with each of my steps and when I enter the class and see Miss Esperanza, when I give her my special smile and she returns one of her own, I imagine that she too could love me, she could love me secretly in her own way, that our age difference is neither here nor there, so I leave my grandson with her and hand her his schoolbag and just as I'm leaving I turn to gaze at her lovingly, knowing that I shall be seeing her later on when I go and pick the boy up for lunch.

Then I walk slowly towards the Roundabout and hear the Postie rattling as it comes to the bend in the road, but instead of running off, I stop by the school railings, take out one of the cigarettes my doctor has banned and I look towards the window just as Esperanza bends down to kiss my grandson, first his forehead, then his cheeks and finally his lips, without taking her eyes off me. Then I throw the cigarette away and rush off just as the bus driver steps on the accelerator, in vain.

Will the Owner of the Salami Step Forward

The normal students have a lot of work to get through. A copious, soporific text. Followed by a literary commentary. Poor things. The three quarters of an hour will barely even give them enough time to get started, ha, ha.

A completely different matter is the little group in the back. Seven feisty pupils who become impossible on days of storm clouds or when the easterly blows. What's more, three of them are real lost cases, far too hardened for their age. Theirs have fourteen, fifteen and sixteen springs, all conscientiously sharpened. The teacher's is automatic; bedsprings, he has let slip on occasion in the teachers' room, scandalizing the new English teacher most of all.

A literary commentary in the last period; what a way to screw someone's morning up. That's what one of the three musketeers mutters, the one who can hold the teacher's stare for longest.

In any case, after giving them a few succinct instructions, they all set about the task, each sector in its own little way. Three sectors in all: the normal students, the rabble and the teacher. The teacher himself is, on his own merits, a complete sector, one whole side. The clearest difference between all the sectors is that two of them, much to their regret, are still completely beardless while the third group, just by running his hand over his cheeks, can feel that his chin is already beginning to get bristly after forgetting to shave for three days. The unpremeditated stubble makes quite a contrast with the fuzz of the sector that is up in arms.

Yes, it is a good way to screw someone's morning up, making them do a literary commentary in the last period, but so what?

Sometimes, as he observes the disciplined stillness of his more outstanding students, their exemplary manners, if he ever stops to think about it, it strikes him that they are more foolish than the others; seeing them there almost nailed to their seats makes him wonder why they don't rebel even in the slightest against such a gross act of injustice. Then again, if he considers that the literary commentary has come straight after a very long hour's worth of introduction to biochemistry, his first appraisal changes radically. The teacher then infers that such submissiveness may be quite normal, and that it is probably quite natural that some of them are dozing off as they read the text, which is all blurred due to the bad quality of the photocopies. It just seems paradoxical that they should deem it fair to be faced with such an outrageous punishment, duty or inanity, as if it were some kind of balsam.

What's going on over there in the corner? Poker is strictly forbidden after the last altercation, but not card games in general, so they are perfecting new ways of betting with other Heraclio Fournier decks. Surprisingly, the new cards are still unmarked after a few hours.

I bid.

I pass.

There's a loud whispering spreading across the classroom from those desks at the back, a mumble which, eventually, when left to its own will, usually ends up becoming an inoffensive, otherwise monotonous murmur. The sound values of such a murmur could doubtless be measured in decibels, but it would be easier to say that they vary between the sound made by a pet tabby cat and one made by a concrete mixer of a cubic metre and a half, or some such. It all depends on the victories, the teacher's expression and the permissiveness of both sectors.

It is, quite obviously, as the teacher has all too often set out to the rest of his colleagues, a matter of rowdy poetics which is very easy to keep in hand, and which at the same time allows the school to save systematically on photocopying. However, his pedagogical strategy is strongly criticised at every staff meeting for being atypical, risky and provocative.

It will not be the last time the scene is repeated: the new English teacher's eyes brimful of blue are the only abstention in a thicket of raised arms. There may be other hidden arguments behind these votes, which is what the teacher suspects, but it's probably best, he considers in turn, to act the fool once again and hold his ground without prying. For the moment the divergence is so evident, so overwhelming, that the hands against him all rise like a wave around the table in a second pointless round that the deputy head proposed in order to gloat a bit longer. So the general implementation of such methods in the classrooms is once more condemned.

In order to soften the bitter aftertaste, and without any ulterior motives whatsoever, the secretary, who has a say, but not a vote in the whole matter, gives the teacher a copy of a collection of poems by Miguel d'Ors, <u>Advanced Course in Ignorance</u>. They both laugh.

Do his colleagues really have no inkling whatsoever of the advantages of turning the tables? If they are not allowed to play dice or cards, those seven kids would spend their time, as the record shows, vilely disrupting the class. In fact they do disrupt the chemistry and drawing classes, the history and mathematics classes, all the ones that are not his. His colleagues might well conceive, then, as it does not require much intelligence, that the relative peace of the armistice in the classroom generates a space for production at other levels.

"If they aren't able to sense it," as the

secretary assures the teacher taking him to one side, "it may be because the staff is too concerned with the rumpus of the legality or illegality of the approach; their earflaps are so correct, so to speak, that they are unable to see what's at either side." A clever man, that secretary. "The armed faction's mis-appropriation of lessons," he adds, clearing his throat on the way to the canteen, "allows the more exemplary pupils a fuller use of the minutes of each lesson. It only remains to transmit the idea in two or three words, which would become a slogan: gamblers in the corner, distinctions in the first row; something along those lines, but even shorter."

Simultaneously, his pupils might presume that the teacher is also dozing over a blank sheet of paper, that about half way through the lesson, having automatically scrawled a moderately huge number of abstract doodles on it, he ends up dropping off completely. But that is exactly what he wishes to show on the outside. During his little nap the teacher keeps working on low revs. He is ticking over, thinking and structuring a project that is still vague, while out of the corner of his eye he can see that some of his pupils are reading, or have gone straight into the commentary after skimming over the first photocopies, while others are paying up, or calling it quits or getting paid.

By now, the teacher's pituitary perceives it very clearly: the fragrance of a shameless, greasy piece of pork meat slowly invades the classroom. Only the counterattack, less covert than one would desire, of twenty-something pairs of trainers along with their equivalent in scented socks, manages to conceal ever so slightly what is going to happen next. Maybe his colleagues are right in refusing: our neck, our integrity is constantly on the line. Those projectiles, besides, are not launched unless they are well past their sell-by date.

But there is still enough time in the last period for each sector to be able to defend its position.

The teacher's psychological barricade, in its blatant hieroglyphic format, is not lacking in substance. Those doodles must be looked at carefully, for if you try and find any meaning in them, they end up looking more like automatic discharges of ink than anything else. Only once the eye gets used to them and manages to discard the twaddle which is expressed in two kinds of lines, the basic lines to gather momentum and the secondary lines more typical of the art of disguise, can it see that the rest of the page shelters an almost schizophrenic series of sketches of building tops, roofs, bizarre models of gabled, apex and hipped roofs.

However, since he has put them down on paper rather than on the blackboard it all looks rather motlier than on other occasions and much more difficult to interpret. Even the teacher himself would have a hard time explaining what the hell he meant to express with the drawing of those springs, whether what he had in mind was bedsprings, weapons or just plain tension.

The fact is you cannot turn your back on the class for even one minute, not even metaphorically speaking. Hence the need to scribble his prolix architectural notes on a vulgar piece of paper. It would be stupid of him to jeopardize the tacit agreement reached soon after the year began.

Maybe at the very end of the class, in the last minutes perhaps, he will pluck up courage and venture out into the dangerous territory of the blackboard and use one of the chalk stubs to draw some of his spectacular sketches, camouflaged with some or other code that will allow the pupils to confront the literary commentary properly tomorrow. It's a risk he ought to take.

The empty rubbish bags, of course, have been visibly arranged next to his table since first thing this morning. Having such a decoy ready at all times is a minor concession that is not too much trouble for a teacher. Some time ago it was no effort at all for him to spend some minutes after class picking up the perpetual paper planes and tin foil balls —aimed at the framed head of state on the wall— the pieces of chalk and plasticine. So it's no skin off his nose to pick up such a fine collection of pork products, practically the whole contents of the most select sandwiches, the raging novelty of these louts.

The secret fantasy of the teacher (to blow up the school building and build one to suit his own needs) is even more dangerous and yet there it is in the middle of his classroom, on his desk, hidden among all the other sketches, as if so much planning were merely a symptom of his educational boredom. It is an intricate project. The best way to lay out the volley so that the building falls in one go, in any case, is not something the teacher loses any sleep over at night; he is more concerned about whether they'd allow him to rebuild it afterwards, as he is no more than an amateur at architectural design, completely self-taught.

The new English teacher must have found out about it by now. Enemies find it hard to keep quiet. He can just imagine them in the canteen, mentioning his case in passing, slipping it in among other trivial anecdotes, making damn sure they did as much damage as they possibly could. They must have told her the same old joke: the one about the linguistics teacher, ha, ha, he's a double loser, a quantity surveyor and mathematician interruptus retrained to become a third-rate philologist. A joke which is all right, even amusing, thinks the teacher, when it is he who is telling it humorously, but not even remotely funny when it is told by other tongues and intentions.

The teacher, however, has no choice but to make a very different reading of that disaster: choosing to drop out of a degree in architecture and then one in exact sciences before it was too late gave him no end of advantages back then and he considers that he by no means lost them all when he finally settled for a minor degree in language and literature. For example, he can walk in the clouds whenever he wishes to, builds roofs with no foundations, roofs that are held up by furious constellations of stains, at the mere expense of his enthusiasm and a felt-tip pen and every morning, when he reaches the school and contemplates the building front on, he wonders out loud whether the architect shouldn't die of embarrassment after making such a botch of it.

That's where he touches a real raw nerve with his colleagues, who are in compelled cahoots with the drawing teacher, a complete half-wit who has been acting as deputy head for some years now.

Academic life.

In short, life.

When there is no space to squeeze

absolutely anything else onto the sheet of paper, the teacher stands up, without meaning to incite anyone.

From a previous class, all mixed up with complicated biochemistry formulas, are some scribbles in English on the blackboard. The teacher is well aware that those words must have an exact translation, but languages were never his forte. However, withstanding the tension of the last few minutes and sensing that some of his pupils have started separating their bread from its filling, he is very pleased to discover that she uses coloured chalk to teach and now that he has his back turned to the pandemonium, he can delight in words of obscure meaning written in green, yellow, orange and blue, which finally end up spattered with pieces of mortadella, projectiles of olives and old cheese, like on other memorable occasions.

It's a ritual that has been going on for a term now. Since the day of the salami, when the teacher turned around infuriated and challenged the perpetrator, having no clue who it had been, to come out to the blackboard, it he had any balls.

"Not balls, salami," he remembers the youth saying firmly that morning as he stepped forward, one of the members of the feisty pupils, one of the three lost cases, the ringleader of them all, his own son. "Not balls, salami, just salami." He can still hear the reply, dry and painful in his head. He doubts he will ever forget it.

Now, these days, after wielding his automatic, as he spikes the slabs of pork meat and puts them in the bag, father and son observe each other in silence. The teacher has no idea what the boy must be thinking. He wishes he could ask him. What he can see, however, is that the layer of fuzz on his son's upper lip is getting thicker by the day, and that he still hasn't dared shave it off. He must be following his mother's advice. She has spent the last two years shacked up with that half-wit architect cum drawing teacher who goes around acting as deputy head; his mother, the same woman who for some time has been finding it harder and harder to bear the thought of her ex-husband going for regular strolls with the new English teacher.

The Latest Mishaps

Dawn has not yet broken. In fact, until the clocks change back, it will be getting light later and later. There are undoubtedly many advantages of having a planet that revolves around the sun and around itself, but there are obviously some deplorable capitulations involved: having to switch on the headlights when the bulb of one of them has been blown for ages; having to start the day, so early, squinting and reckless behind a steering wheel. Unless Octavio decides to risk turning them on full beam, knowing that although they diverge, they are at least intact and light the way.

Besides, it's raining, it's bucketing, it's

raining the contents of a storm more characteristic of the end of the dry season than the beginning of autumn. Although all the hours of the 21st have come and gone, the staff on the meteorology payroll is reluctant to inaugurate it officially. Octavio, however, forces himself to put the windscreen wipers on medium speed, after having turned on the ignition and set off, with his briefcase and a pathetic screwdriver on the passenger seat, a seat devoid of a co-driver as of today.

In order to get to work, Octavio has to go around half a dozen roundabouts, three of which are decorated with strategic traffic lights. The other three are lacking in electronic scarecrows, minor roundabouts backstitched with a few panels re-commending drivers to slow down and give way to those coming out of the corner of their eye. One of them, besides, is an intersection which fancies itself as something special, as it has an acceleration lane, the roundabout which Octavio takes every day in order to get to the main ring road of the city, that inadequate thoroughfare signposted with generous blue panels which every now and then promise the opportunity of being able to reach all, absolutely all directions. "All roads lead to Rome," their reflective letters could argue.

Octavio has to leave countless signposts behind every morning before he gets to work. "All roads lead to Rome," he mumbles as he passes them, using the expression to depict a stylised variant of the most mundane of facts, which is that each morning, all roads lead to the industrial estate where he works.

Maybe today will be different. There are reasons and signs that provide evidence that it may be so, as far as he can see: the storm, the unusual company in the co-driver's seat, the loud raindrops dripping from the overhead signposts onto the bodywork of his car...

As soon as he started the car he sensed

the traffic jam in all its magnitude. For the moment the traffic is still moving along the four lanes, but at little more than ten kilometres an hour, on the verge of coming to a total standstill. And what's that winking over there behind the impenetrable blackness? In the distance the square roots of the bolts of lightning are committing suicide, followed by claps of thunder and intermittent blasts of the horns of the vehicles of large tonnage which portend an immense traffic jam.

Octavio switches on the radio just as the announcer is saying the words "with a large electrical appliance". He turns the dial but he cannot find any substantial differences between one station and the next. He turns it off. He would rather deal with the raging horns, the ineffectual symphonic strategy of the raindrops on the roof. How sweetly irresponsible it would be now for Octavio, had he not given up months ago, to fill his lungs with a cigarette, a whole packet!

The traffic has almost ground to a halt. According to the speedometer on his dashboard, his speed —after all he is still moving— is negligible.

Then Octavio turns, and without looking at it directly, glances at the seat next to him, empty, with the briefcase and the screwdriver in the place that was otherwise occupied by Alejandra until just yesterday.

Of course he should have put that tool back where it belonged long ago. Octavio's toolbox is almost as clumsy as his hands, but Octavio has never tried to conceal the fact. However, he has hammers, lots of spanners, nuts, washers, even sanding paper and a set of screwdrivers of every conceivable size. It is due to the lack of imagination of his elders, who every Christmas unfailingly give him socks, lighters (!) and tools. And one of them has made it to the co-pilot's seat today, the braggart.

It's true that even people who are useless

45

at DIY often have to deal with some little repairs around the house, fitting new plugs, changing the odd tap, oiling hinges. But once the domestic repairs and disrepairs have been seen to, and this is the biggest mistake, Octavio tends to leave his tacks and pliers lying around any old where, that huge screwdriver on top of the music shelf. How many days has he eyed it with certain apprehension as he heard stories of abuse, war and conflicts on the news?

"Please put that provocation back in its box," Alejandra would beg him on days of implausible fights ("The fact that you are an only child, Octavio, and you'll have to excuse me, but it's a monstrous aberration." "In my worst nightmares, Alexia, I find you laughing at the stupid little jokes of your seven dense brothers in-law, all of whom are older brothers of mine".), on days of subsequent silent bewilderment.

If only he had put that tool back in time. What's more, the box should have been in the flat and not in the boot of the car, always parked miles away, four, eight, twelve blocks from the house. That's why this morning, with the rain pelting down, Octavio hasn't had the chance to put it in the boot and has placed it next to the briefcase on the empty co-driver's seat. Things aren't looking too bright: a huge traffic jam and Octavio is in possession of a sharp instrument with a caramel-coloured handle, with no cigarettes or Alejandra to hold his anxiety in place.

As the general bulk of the jam enters the bottleneck of other roundabouts, the traffic slows down even more, if such a thing were possible, all that horsepower going to waste, flushed faces behind steamed-up windows. And dawn is still not willing to break.

There is a crack and a boom and everything finally stops, permanently.

It takes a while for his eyes and ears to recover and see and hear that what is going on a bit further along the road looks like several vehicles strewn across the tarmac. They all flaunt garlands of revolving blue lights. Maybe an accident or some improbable roadblock. It's going to take a while; it may even get light.

Octavio makes his mind up. Like other daring drivers, who don't seem to mind the downpour, he gets out of his car. Yet Octavio has no intention of finding out what's going on. Certain that the rain will wash away any redness remaining from the latest mishaps, he drives the screwdriver clean through the tyres and walks off, without an umbrella, in search of all directions.

Andrés Neuman

Visitors' Book

*A*ndrés Neuman *(Buenos Aires, 1977) lives in Granada, where he graduated in Hispanic Philology. He has lectured in Latin American literature, has several press columns, writes comic strips and cultivates different literary genres. He has had three collections of short stories published, El que espera (He who waits), El último minuto (The Last Minute) and Alumbramiento (Birth), and an anthology about contemporary short-story writing called Pequeñas Resistencias (Small Resistances). He is the author of the novels Bariloche (Bariloche), La Vida en las ventanas (The Life in Windows), which was short-listed for the Primavera Prize and Una vez Argentina (Once Argentina), short-listed for the Herralde Prize. Included in the most important anthologies on young Spanish poetry, he has published several collections of poems: Métodos de la Noche (Night Methods), El jugador de billar (The Pool Player), El tobogán (The Slide) and La canción del antílope (The Antilope's Song). He has also developed his skills in haiku in Gotas Negras (Black Drops) and aphorism, in El equilibrista (The Tightrope Walker).*

He says that he wrote this story, Visitors' Book, after a hectic night in a hotel. The incidents inspired a story about a man who receives disturbing anonymous notes in every hotel he stays in, notes which will gradually reveal his identity.

50

Visitors' Book

My identity is irrelevant now and in any case, it is not in my interest to reveal it. Let's just say that for work reasons I frequently sleep, or should I say I do not sleep, in hotels.

This whole thing started some months back, I cannot remember the exact date, at a hotel reception desk. I was handed a magnificent gold pen, or at least that was what I was told, a gold pen with which to imprint my name and, if I was kind enough, a comment regarding the hotel or at least a dedication. And that is just what I was about to do, grasping the pen with disinterest and haughtiness, not out of conceit but rather because I could not honestly think of anything to write. I was tired, I sleep badly and I was trying to save time. The receptionist sensed my uneasiness and slipped discreetly over to the counter, leaving me alone. I seized the opportunity to browse through some previous dedications and try and find some inspiration in them. It was then, having reached the last entry in the book, that I came across the following message:

"What a disappointing experience I have just had in the bar. A glass of brandy at that price, even if it is a vintage Napoleon, is a complete swindle. In the hotel Plaza, in the Sheraton, at the top of the damn Empire State Building or the Eiffel Tower the same brandy would cost less. Do not forget that stinginess also has a price and besides being unseemly, it is bad business. If you charged reasonable prices, in accordance with the category of the hotel, of course, yet reasonable, the guests would be delighted to have a second and third brandy, I am sure. I will never again consume any kind of drink in this hotel and I shall advise everyone I know to do likewise. Not because I cannot afford to, but because I hate being cheated. Sincerely, N. N."

That was the note I found and that was what it said. I was surprised it was in the visitors' book and not in the complaints book. Maybe the person who wrote it thought it better to make his observation as public as possible, to make sure all the important figures staying at the hotel were aware of it, in a spirit of revenge. It was possible. The fact is that the note confused me, I cannot really say why, and prevented me from being able to concentrate on the dedication that I was supposed to write. So after a few perplexed minutes, a couple of coughs and another useless pause, I confined myself to imprinting my signature (in big letters with my name printed in block capitals) and then closed the visitors' book, smiled brusquely at the receptionist and withdrew to my room.

I will not lie by saying that I thought about it the next day because the truth is I completely forgot about it. My meetings and public engagements sucked me into my usual whirl of activity, leaving me exhausted and my consciousness clouded over. But you will probably believe me if I tell you that when I was given the visitors' book in the next hotel in the next city and they begged me to honour them etcetera, etcetera, I could not help but remember N. N. Of course, and I think I should clarify this, I did not suspect for a moment that I would find him there again. On the contrary, it was a vague thought, a kind of intersection, like a penguin which distracts you for a moment from what you are doing and makes you avert your eyes for a few seconds before getting on with your work and banishing it from your mind. And that was how it happened, I just thought, "Ah, N. N." It was just a sigh. That was all. That's why when I read his initials again I was surprised twice, o doubly. I was surprised because of the peculiarity of the note and on the other hand, because I had forgotten all about it and had remembered it again suddenly.

The note said:

"The intrusiveness of the cleaners is inadmissible. I can understand that anyone can make a careless mistake and might open the door first thing in the morning and accidentally wake one of the guests up. But to hear them rattling the door handles all day long, even in the early hours of the morning, or to come back and find one's suitcases changed around goes beyond what is minimally acceptable. If your intention is to invade your guests' intimacy, I would suggest that you fire your cleaners and contract some professional spies, who would be more efficient and would be able to give you more precise information. Sincerely yours, N. N."

On that occasion, after my initial astonishment and temporary speechlessness, my first instinct was to draw the receptionist's attention to the message or at least ask who was behind those initials. But on second thoughts I dismissed the idea because it seemed ungainly. I was embarrassed to alert them to something so distasteful. I was afraid that it would appear as if I endorsed the complaint (and indeed I was aware of the cleaners making a racket in the hall at the break of day) and in any case, I knew that if I did mention the message, all the staff in the hotel would be falling over themselves to make wearisome apologies and they would keep me in reception until they had given me every imaginable excuse about the matter. So once again I kept quiet. I inscribed my signature in large letters and went up to my room. To not sleep.

What can I say now? That I did not give it another thought? That I remembered the incident a couple of times like a group of penguins that passes by, distracting your attention, and then vanishes from your mind? Both things would be true. I believe I thought about it, but with no intensity, with no intention. As if, more than invoking N. N., I had seen him pass before my eyes on a couple of occasions. No more than that. I had a hectic week, packed with meetings and some street disturbances that had to be nipped in the bud.

Ten days later I went on another trip.

So as not to stand on ceremony, I will confine myself to transcribing the following note I found in the next visitors' book in the next hotel after the staff had made a special point of lavishing me with all sorts of kindness and reverences:

"It is very good of you to offer your guests the discreet and anonymous possibility of choosing films of pornographic content. However, it would be nice if the walls were slightly thicker or better still, soundproofed. Hearing pounding noises and groans from an adjoining room is always bothersome (yet understandable), but having to deal with the mechanical, overacted and repetitive howls of a dubbed film of this nature is a nuisance that strikes me as completely unnecessary. Thank you. Yours sincerely, N. N."

I think that the receptionists, who were looking at me with expectation and with their fingers solicitously intertwined, noticed that I was blushing and thought, fortunately, that their presence inhibited me. So they moved away a bit, leaving me alone with the visitors' book. Alone with those messages which quite clearly could not be coincidental.

I pondered over the matter. Was the person following me? Did he have access to my schedule and then made sure he stayed in the same hotels as I did? Despite my bodyguard keeping my rooms under strict surveillance night and day, my hypothesis sent a small shiver down my spine. But most of all, how could he know my every move, my intimate habits so well? And in any case, if he wanted to get in touch with me, why choose such a bizarre way of going about it? Wouldn't it be simpler just to send me a letter, an e-mail, a telegram? The next thing that came to my mind, though more improbable, was even more alarming: was I following him? Was I trailing him without realizing it? Was he having the same thoughts? However, ruling out the coincidence of so many coincidences, I had no way of knowing his movements, his dates, his hotels. How was I supposed to keep abreast of what he was doing if I can barely keep up with what happens around me, let alone know where I am going to sleep, or why I sleep, or anything?

The recurrence of those furtive messages at least confirmed something that I had always suspected. Nobody ever reads the entries in visitors' books, least of all those in charge of hotels. Despite the pains taken over the presentation, the solemn ceremony of leaving a note and the supposed importance they are supposed to have, any efforts made are completely futile. The same as constitutions, once they have been written, nobody ever bothers consulting them.

As for N. N., in the same way as he subtly stopped referring to the "guests" and began to refer directly to the "guest", there came a time in the pursuit when his messages began to allude to me quite explicitly. For example, one night I was forced to read the following:

"I would kindly ask hotel management that owing to the foulness of the latest illustrious guest, you should proceed to thoroughly disinfect the bathrooms on the seventh floor. It is a question of public hygiene. Yours gratefully, N. N."

It did not take long, maybe two or three trips more, before the notes became blatantly threatening. N. N. did not even bother talking to the hotel employees about me, but rather addressed me quite brazenly and with total impunity. People should read visitors' books. I assume that is what they are there for. But nobody was saying anything. And I, naturally, was keeping very quiet. During one of my sleepless nights I lay awake figuring out the progression of the notes. It was as if at first N. N. had meant to attract my attention with impersonal notes that would not compromise him in any way but would undoubtedly arouse my interest, thus making sure that I would always read any visitors' book I was offered. Then he used that to send me personal messages. N. N. knew full well that I was trapped. I could not stop reading the messages but I could never tell the hotel staff about them, either. Quite the opposite, bearing in mind the indecorous revelations that some of them contained, my main interest was to ensure that they were never read. The worst thing was (and to top it all I strongly suspected this was his plan all along) the humiliation of having to raise my eyes from the book and smile, be pleasant and pretend everything was fine. I never mentioned any of this to my bodyguards because to be quite honest, I felt a bit ashamed about it and because I did not want to come across as nervous or unbalanced at a time in which my detractors were accusing me of going astray. And as for the option of not signing the books, there were two reasons that prevented me from doing so. First of all, there were the formal responsibilities of my post and the interests of my fragile public image; secondly, my irrepressible curiosity.

I did not always find the admonitions on the last page of the visitors' books. Obviously, he gave himself a reasonable amount of time; let's say between one and three days. However, towards the end of the book I would always come across the ineluctable messages, which were getting ever shorter and ever more treacherous.

"Why don't you privatize your mansions?"

"Ask your wife what she gets up to while you're away."

"What kind of decision can you make when your right-hand man betrays you? What a pity."

"Do you really think anyone believed the speech you gave yesterday morning?"

"The judiciary should not be treated as room service."

"I hope it goes well for your daughter in the clinic. It could happen to anyone. Even catholic fanatics."

That is what they said, and more. Everything else happening around me, inside and outside the hotel, was the same old predictable stuff. There were no significant changes in my professional or personal life. But N. N.'s messages were as accurate as darts. Sometimes when I was left alone in a room to sign, I would unabashedly rip out the page in the visitors' book before calmly writing my own dedication. I became more anxious about the inscriptions in the visitors' books than what the headlines were saying. Nevertheless, as I have already mentioned, my everyday routine went on as usual. At least until the day in which the message simply told me to:

"Clean my boots. N. N."

That was it. It did not mention a date or a time. Was he being sarcastic? For some reason, I sensed from the beginning that he was not. I signed the visitors' book (I was now used to ripping out pages quite calmly and then leaving long, laudatory passages) and went upstairs, and to be honest, I was not really surprised to find those unfamiliar, black worn-out boots at the foot of my bed. I sighed and looked around me, then inspected the room knowing that there would be no one there. Finally I sat down on the bed for a moment and realized I had no choice.

From then on, the orders became worse. What struck me the most was that the messages never contained explicit threats or mentioned any kind of reprisal if the orders were not carried out. Yet far from reassuring me, it terrified me even more. Whoever was doing this had to be very sure of his own strength and his contacts to know that I, no less than I, would obey. The fact is that although some of the demands were strange, they were never dangerous per se and they never stopped me from carrying out my daily activity as usual. At first I felt humiliated. Then, like most other people I suppose, I got used to living like this.

The more orders I have obeyed, the more has been asked of me. Lately in every message there are two, three and even four clauses that may be related but are never too difficult to perform. I just do them and keep quiet. Everything else is under control. My position seems safe, order is guaranteed and my family is calm. But N. N.'s notes keep following me wherever I go with the same imperiousness in every hotel, in every city, at every moment before I go up to my room to toss and turn in my bed, to open and close my eyes and see the same darkness, to listen to the hum of the air conditioning that so reminds me of a flock of birds, to ask myself some things I cannot reveal here, to wonder if it might not be a bad idea to have a glass of brandy before I drop off, if I manage to, that is.

Margarita Borrero

The Good Woman

Margarita Borrero was born in Barranquilla, Colombia, in 1969. She graduated in Journalism and has worked as a reporter in Colombia, the United States and Spain. She is currently doing a doctorate in Literature in the Universidad Autónoma de Madrid. "The hardest thing about journalism," she has written, "is when the news moves you and yet you are forced to subject it to a professional straitjacket. Where I come from, drug dealers build submarines in the heart of mountain ranges, cemeteries are growing so outrageously that they are invading people's back yards and hired killers appeal to the Virgin, begging for their bullets not to miss. Under these circumstances it is normal to feel that everything that goes on, everything possible, is implausible."

The Good Woman *is the story of a little girl who grew up convinced she was Carlos Gardel's daughter.*

The Good Woman

I grew up convinced that Carlos Gardel was my father. On the wall of our boarding house there was a photo of him which my mother would blow a kiss to every night before going out to earn a living all dressed up in her glad rags. After she had left, I would get up on tiptoe at the head of the bed and unhook the photo and then fall asleep with the image of him in my arms. If it was a bad night and my mum came home in the small hours without a tango on her lips, she would remove it from my embrace, trying her best not to wake me, and she would hang it back on the wall saying: "Oh, Gardel, daddy, if only you could be here with us!"

That image of him with his hat placed firmly on his head had always been there, smiling, and for many years it was my mother's treasure. Then came the gramophone and that soon became our most prized possession. It was a portable, wind-up Colibrí gramophone the colour of red wine. Mum came home with it in her arms early one morning and she was so happy that she woke me up so we could listen to *Caminito* together. In fact we couldn't because the Colibrí was missing its needle —or beak as I called it— and it was almost a month before Mima, an expert at black-market junk shops and unrepentant wearer of the most ridiculous hats, managed to get her hands on one.

We eventually got it going in February 1935, which coincided with the news of Gardel's visit to Bogotá. The girls in the boarding house considered the news a good enough reason to have a never-ending party and just to make things a little livelier, my

mother and I decided to christen the
gramophone in style, or rather its needle.
We took it down to the ground floor and
put it in the patio, right in the middle of the
old colonial building. I remember that
morning as being unusually hot and I ended
up with a sore arm after having to wind up
the gramophone so many times. The first
song picked up speed slowly and it was very
moving to hear *Mano a mano* because the
girls all considered it a kind of hymn.

Deranged by my sadness
You come into my mind and I realize that
you have been
In my poor pariah's life
Just a good woman.
Your stylish presence
Put warmth in my nest,
You were good, consistent
And I know that you have loved me
The way you have never loved before
The way you will never be able to love
again.

That irresistible voice brought all the women out onto their balconies in their see-through dressing gowns, their miniskirts and their red lingerie. Mari, the youngest one, came out stark naked and rested her forearms and breasts on the rail and then started to sing as if she was a summer swallow and Bogotá was the warmest city in the world. When Hortensia made a rude remark, Mari replied quite casually that tangos were sung much better without any clothes on. It was so funny that from then on it became a custom in the boarding house for the girls to make as if to take all their clothes off as soon as they heard Gardel's voice. That first afternoon we played the gramophone they sang the songs over and over for hours on end, totally unselfconsciously, such was the bewitching effect my daddy's voice had on them. My daddy who wasn't my daddy, of course, but that happy morning on which the balconies were filled with songbirds, I was still not aware of it.

What I was aware of was that he was going to perform in the Royal Theatre on the 10th of June and there was only one way I was going to be able to see him. I offered to polish the boarding-house girls' shoes for fifty cents a pair and after shining twenty pairs of ankle boots, sixty pairs of high heels and five pairs of boots, I managed to raise the forty-two pesos I needed for two front-row seats and the taxi fare to and from the theatre. My mother looked magnificent that evening. She wore her most elegant suit and Mima's best hat just to add a Gardelian touch, which made us laugh. All of the twenty-five girls who lived in the boarding house all clucked around her like hens in a coop, and set about doing her make-up, hair and perfume. They did the same with me but when they had finished, my mother gave me a quick once-over and decided that I was plastered in too much make-up. She smeared a piece of toilet paper with some

Ponds make-up remover and rubbed it all over my face, despite the girls' vociferous protests, and I had no choice but to go to the concert adorned only with my green velvet suit and red eyes because of the Ponds cream. Once we were seated, the redness only got worse because I wept through each of those tangos. I am unable to describe the feeling his breathtakingly beautiful voice aroused in me. Mum and I left the theatre arm in arm, singing *El día que me quieras* chorused by a group of drunks. We were absolutely convinced that our happiness was indestructible and would last forever.

At about five o'clock on the afternoon of the 24th of June, I looked up from my homework and saw a huge black feather moving diagonally across the patio and coming towards us. It was the hat Mima kept for the saddest occasions. She opened the door without even knocking and I felt a shiver run down my spine when I saw the distraught look on her face. My mother, who was sewing the hem on one of her tango skirts, jumped up when she saw her come in, dropping her box of buttons and her needle and thread, which all clattered to the floor after bouncing off the toe of her black shoes.

"Did you hear the news?" asked Mima.

We hadn't heard the news but by the expression on her face we knew that it was bad. We shook our heads at the same time and were on the verge of fainting at the same time when those fleshy lips, painted the colour of dry blood uttered the three words that would brusquely change the course of my life.

"Gardel is dead."

"What do you mean?"

"A plane accident. Two hours ago. When he was taking off from Medellín."

Nobody cried his death like we did because nobody in the world loved him as much or had felt him so theirs. For days and nights all of our arms did shifts to keep the gramophone playing in the middle of the patio with the sole purpose of letting its needle tear our hearts to shreds. We all agreed that the songs sounded even more poignant after the accident and there simply weren't enough handkerchiefs in all the boarding house that could soak up the tears we shed over Gardel. When the needle of our Colibrí finally snapped and it looked as if we were going to have to live without the music we needed to keep tormenting ourselves, Mari brought a friend of hers who played the accordion in the bar where she worked, and even though he played quite badly, he helped us fill our afternoons with tangos until our voices faded along with that year of 1935, tattooed on our souls like the scar of a cigarette that has been stubbed out on skin.

My mother did not get around to mourning the first anniversary of my father's death, but only by a whisker.

Towards the end of May 1936 she had a bout of flu which then turned into pneumonia. However, she was able to anticipate her tragic ending. When she realized her strength was waning she called Mima, whispered something in her ear, to which Mima nodded before walking briskly past me and into her bedroom. She left the house with her brown hat on, which she wore when she was visiting someone important. I spent the rest of the afternoon by my mother's side. I only got up to close the window when I realized it had started raining diagonally, which only happens in Bogotá when a tragic ending is approaching. Through one of the panes I saw Mima arriving with a man dressed in a black striped suit. I was moved to see how hard he was trying to shelter her with his umbrella, but he was so thin that the wind was dragging him away and she had to hold on to his arm so he wouldn't fly off. I unlocked the door and sat back down on the bed. They came in dripping wet. He greeted us both with a nod of his head and pulled a chair over to sit down beside me. Soon afterwards I was left alone with him and my mother because Mima went to light the stove and make some coffee. The first gesture of that man, who wore a side parting like all good *milongueros,* was to run his hand over my head.

"It this her?" he asked. He had a gentle, well-modulated voice which was enough to make me like him instantly.

"It is. Her name is Ana María but everyone calls her *La Gardelita.*"

Then my mum clasped my hands in hers, stared at me gravely and said:

"This is your father. His name is Pastor."

That was how I found out that Carlos Gardel was not the author of my days. I was nine years old when I went to live with Pastor, who taught mathematics in a state school. Years later I discovered that it was the only matrimonial parenthesis my mother had ever made, and yet I never found out why or under what circumstances they separated. To his credit, I must say that he was careful never to speak badly of her in front of me. He paid for all the funeral costs and offered me a safe home and a good education. However, he did not want me to return to the neighbourhood where I grew up and would not allow any of the girls to come and see me, either. I saw Mima only once, two months after my mother's funeral. The poor thing arrived panting with the gramophone in her arms. She had sent it to be repaired and had also brought a box-full of needles so that I would never run out again. Finally she handed me some of Carlos Gardel's records which she said she had found, although I was sure, because I knew her too well, that she had invested all her savings in them. I made her sit on one of the worn-out Louis XV armchairs in Pastor's living room and then, with a gesture that almost seemed magic, she wound up the Colibrí so that we could listen to *Mano a mano* together for the last time.

> *Meanwhile, may your victories,*
> *Your poor fleeting victories,*
> *Become a long line*
> *Of riches and pleasure;*
> *And may the moneybags who takes you in*
> *Have long-lasting cash*
> *And may you flaunt your vanity*
> *Among pimping milongueros*
> *And may the boys all say*
> *"She is a good woman."*

We took leave of each other in floods of tears and she told me we would never see each other again but that she was sure that my studies would make me become a respectable woman. She was wrong, but only partly. It's hardly surprising that I chose to study music and then became a teacher, like Pastor. The truth is that Mima and I did see each other again. Twenty years had gone by and although for Gardel they may have been nothing, seeing them in Mima's excessive wrinkles and near baldness was devastating. I went to see her in a charity-funded hospital where she was dying of a bout of syphilis she had not been able to shake off. A nurse had found an old scrunched up piece of paper with my address and phone number on it in her bag and had been good enough to contact me.

On my second visit I took the gramophone along with me and the patients in the wing all seemed to spring to life that afternoon when they heard *Adiós muchachos*. The following afternoon, *Por una cabeza*. And then *Mi Buenos Aires Querido*. They sang until my arm ached because I had not wound up the Colibrí for ages and was out of practice. During one of my chats with Mima I told her about the new record players that worked with electricity and which sounded a thousand times better than the old gramophone but she just discredited what I had said with an irrefutable argument: "Carlitos sings better and better every day; but to understand that, you have to listen to him with all the noise of Buenos Aires in the background."

I buried her next to my mother and every week I go and change their gardenias. Her epitaph reads the same words that Carlos Gardel said to his audience in Bogotá after his last concert. "I cannot say goodbye, but farewell." Some days I sit by their graves until late and wait until everyone has left the cemetery so that no witness will ever be able to reproach me for what I do. I hum *Sus ojos se cerraron* thinking abut them both because I am sure that if there is any music capable of producing a shiver of passion in the earth of the deceased, it would have to be one of Gardel's tangos.

This whole story is relevant because on the 24th of June of this same year, the fortieth anniversary of Carlitos's death, a journalist followed me home and then published an article with my photo which he titled <u>Gardel's Colombian Daughter</u>. The whole muddle came about because during the commemoration I left a wreath which said: *"To Daddy, in memoriam"*. The reporter, convinced that he was onto the biggest story of his life, has been watching me and delving into my past. He wrote, among other things, that as a child I was called *La Gardelita* and now there is a mob of people at my door night and day asking me whether I really am his daughter.

The answer is no, I am not. It would make a good story for a tango but it is not true. What is true is that he was always in my life and my mother's life with his music for common people and his magical smile and, thanks to him, my childhood was filled with passion. But in order to avoid people asking who my mother was or what she did for a living, or prying into a past which only I have the right to access, I will say the same words that the man I thought for years to be my father would have said. I will say that *her stylish presence / Warmed up my nest, / She was good, consistent / And I know that she loved me / The way she had never loved before / The way she will never be able to love again.*

Guillermo Niño de Guzmán

The Kite

Guillermo Niño de Guzmán was born in Lima in 1955. He studied Linguistics and Literature and graduated with a thesis on the life and work of Ernest Hemingway. He has worked as a journalist and collaborated with several publishers. He has done some literary translations, written film and television scripts, directed jazz programmes and worked as a bullfighting critic. He was a war correspondent in Bosnia and in the 1994 military conflict between Peru and Ecuador. He has lived in Paris, Madrid and Barcelona.

He has published two collections of short stories, <u>Caballos de medianoche</u> (Midnight Horses) and <u>Una mujer no hace un verano</u> (One woman does not make a summer) and a historical novel called <u>El tesoro de los sueños</u> (The Treasure of Dreams).

He admits that when he writes he tries to imitate the epic and sentimental styles of Tolstoy, Stendhal and Gógol, the concise and direct style of Hemingway; the introspective intention of Malcolm Lowry, in order to delve into man's darkest urges that will lead him to hell and back in search of his real identity.

The Kite

> The darkness would not protect him. He was to enter a night of innumerable snares, of changing eyes. He was not sure whether he should do it, whether he should dare.
>
> *James Salter*

Santiago squinted but the shine of the phosphorescent hands and numbers on the clock was too dim for his short-sighted eyes. He had to grasp it and bring it within a hand span of his face in order to verify that it was well gone three o'clock in the morning. He had spent over an hour lying awake in the darkness and his ears were now used to recognizing the sounds that broke the silence of the night. His wife's breathing as he lay by her side was calm and steady. Through the open window came a light breeze which made the tulle curtain billow, and when a vehicle came around the corner, its headlights swept over the walls and roof in the bedroom. This only lasted a couple of seconds. Then he would hear the hum of the engine which got louder as it passed the house followed by a change in gear the driver would make before accelerating and disappearing to the end of the road.

In the distance he could hear a dog's pitiful howl, and when it stopped, Santiago picked up the persistent chirps of a cricket in ambush in the shrubs that grew below the bedroom window. It was quite hot and he had a band of sweat around his neck. Then, supporting himself on his hands and trying not to make any jerky movements, he raised himself to a sitting position. He groped around the bedside table until he found his glasses. His wife was still sleeping soundly and Santiago noticed the beads of perspiration lining her top lip.

He carefully got up from the bed, put on his slippers and moved slowly, so as to avoid bumping into any pieces of furniture. He went into the hall and as he was walking by the room of his son Roberto, who slept with the door open, Santiago stopped for a moment to listen. The boy was snoring, making long, muffled grunts. Then he walked on until he reached the stairs and went down them cautiously, holding on tight to the handrail. He did not wish to switch on the light. He felt more at ease surrounded by darkness.

When he got to the kitchen he opened the fridge and was briefly blinded by the light inside it. He took out a can of ginger ale and rolled it over his sweaty forehead before opening it. He took a long drink and went to get the cigarettes he usually left by the phone. He wasn't at all sleepy. He was about to light up when he was suddenly overcome with a very strange feeling. Something was wriggling in his chest, pounding and pushing as if it wished to get out through his skin. Overcome with a growing feeling of anxiety, he went out onto the back patio and dashed up the spiral staircase that led to the terrace roof.

Once he reached the top of the stairs, while he was getting his breath back, he gazed at the deep, clear sky that seemed to open itself up before him, offering him its dark arms tattooed with tiny stars. His initial exhilaration slowly started to wear off and Santiago was aware of an unfamiliar sense of peace flooding through his whole body. He walked unsteadily over to the low wall that went around the front part of the terrace and sat down with his legs dangling over the edge. He still had the can of drink in his hand but he had mislaid his cigarettes.

He looked around him and saw the roofs of neighbouring houses, the tall buildings that rose up along the nearby avenue and the red lights flickering at the tips of the antennas. Santiago noticed that the night noises had all faded. Nevertheless, something was moving. It was the shadows cast by the trees illuminated by the street lamps. The wind was making the leaves sway gently, creating vague forms that crept silently along the pavement.

What struck him the most was the silence. Not one lonely cry, not one distant siren slicing through the night. It was as if the whole world had stopped still. In the midst of such calm, Santiago perceived a certain vibration in the atmosphere. The breeze was coming off the beach, climbing the wall of the cliff all the way to his rooftop and forcing the warm air to retreat. It was a gentle wind that came and went with a cadence similar to that of the sea. Santiago squinted and let himself be swept along by a surge of lightness. In the distance he heard the reverberation of a deep noise, of regular frequency, which reminded him of a double bass playing the same note over and over again.

Santiago kept his eyelids closed and imagined it was the earth's heartbeat. He breathed in deeply and the smell of the sea and the night came rushing up his nostrils and flooded his lungs. A slight shiver ran down his spine and his hand let go of the can of ginger ale. He opened his eyes and saw it plunging towards the street, a fall which seemed endless, like a film in slow-motion. He followed its descent, watching it bounce off the window sill and every turn it took before crashing against the footpath. The strangest thing was that there was absolutely no sound. The can then leaped along like a balloon, softly, two or three times, until it finally rolled under a car parked in front of his house.

Vaguely entranced, Santiago felt his body relaxing and becoming weightless, as if he had rid himself of a huge burden. A few seconds later he looked down and realized that his body had levitated almost thirty centimetres above the wall. Thinking it was a mirage, he reached down and ran his hand underneath his thighs to confirm whether it was indeed an optical illusion. Yet all he found was air.

What was happening? Now he reached down with both arms and ran them underneath his legs, verifying that he had taken off from where he was sitting. It was unbelievable, but there was no doubt about it. He was suspended in mid air. Had he lost his gravity, like one of those cosmonauts in space? He tried to sit up and instead of landing back on the wall, he was pushed a metre higher. He was floating! Then he felt brave enough to move a foot and his body glided effortlessly forward. He took another step and floated even further away from the rooftop. The weirdest thing of all was that he was not at all afraid of the void, just a little disconcerted. A couple of steps more and he was already halfway across the street. It's not so hard, he thought. He turned his head to the right and his body repeated the movement as if he had pressed some kind of button on a remote control. After a bit more experimenting, he discovered that if he raised his hands above his head he went shooting upwards and if he lowered them he came down.

It did not take long for him to work out that it was much more comfortable for him to float in a horizontal position and that his speed depended on the amount of energy he put into moving his head or limbs. He kept on practising his manoeuvres until he felt ready to go for a little fly. Nothing too risky. He would start by flying around the house.

He set off slowly on his reconnaissance flight, keeping close to the rooftop, the same way those learning to swim cling to the edge of the pool. He went around it carefully, without any mishaps. Then he decided to go down the façade of the house, to the second floor, to the windows of Roberto's room. His son was lying there face up and was still snoring. Why not go in? It was an old building with high ceilings and spacious rooms. It wouldn't be so hard to manoeuvre once he got inside. He slid inside the open window stealthily, waving his hands and arms like a diver. First he glided over the bed and then flew down, hovering half a metre from the floor, before edging his way slowly over to the head of the bed. He could not resist the urge to touch him as he slept and Santiago stroked his son's hair. Roberto was in full adolescence and their relationship was far from being optimal. It was true that the boy had witnessed some of his excesses and, as one would expect from an only child, he acted in complicity with his mother, in direct opposition to his father's extravagant behaviour. Santiago left the room and turned into the hall where he nearly bumped into an overhead lamp that was switched off. He wanted to turn around and go for a fly around his wife's room. What would happen if she woke up? Would she shriek? Or would she try and swat at him as if he were a night blowfly. Santiago smiled. He knew that his wife considered him a little strange, yet not half as much as what other people thought. And if she caught him in full flight, she might run out into the street scared out of her wits.

He flew down until he was hovering over her, so close that he could feel her exhaling. If he woke her up, he suddenly thought, she might realize for once that he was not just your average kind of man. But was it worth it? In all likelihood she would not understand a thing. In any case, he was assailed by a doubt. Would he be allowed to share his gift with others? Or would the spell break, sending him crashing to the floor? Nevertheless, he pondered, what was the point in being able to fly if nobody would ever be able to appreciate it? It was unfair. To have such a marvellous skill and not be able to tell anyone would be frustrating.

Santiago came to the conclusion that he needed proof, something that would vouch for his flight. He remembered that a couple of days back, the wind had sent Roberto's kite hurling into the overhead cables, where it had got stuck. It was a nice kite and his son was very upset about not being able to get it back because he had designed it himself and had taken a lot of pains to make it. From his study window, Santiago had watched the vain attempts of his son and his friends to retrieve it.

Yes, that was a good idea. Roberto would be glad to see that his father was willing to leave all his papers aside and stop annoying everyone with his concerns about his imaginative block in order to go and do something as useful and common as rescuing a stuck kite. Santiago pushed himself out of the room and flew up to the

power lines and took a good look at the
kite, trying to figure out how to cut it loose.
As he had feared, the tail had become even
more entangled due to the continual gusts
of wind. He knew that as long as he did not
touch the ground he would not be in any
danger, but he had to be careful. He decided
to take a short break before proceeding, so
he flew back up to the rooftop and let his
feet rest on the wall.

Santiago felt fulfilled, with an intimate
certainty that he had always been deprived
of. From up there, everything looked
different. The thousand eyes of the night,
tiny and shiny like salamanders, squiggled
around him. He glanced at the vast, clean
sky and for the first time, believed that he
had finally understood the meaning of the
world, the life that hid in the darkness, all of
those muffled cries, all of those angry looks,
all of those longings that spur men on. He
was keeping vigil over the city's sleep and
the night had opened itself up to him and

offered him a huge hand that would pick him up and carry him off through the air.

An instinctive reflex made him turn. He made out a figure a couple of metres away from the wall, camouflaged by the darkness. He adjusted his glasses and saw it was his wife. She was wearing a white dressing gown and was scrutinizing him with a strange expression on her face. Santiago heard a buzzing in his ear and thought it to be a kind of alarm. Yes, it could all go to waste. He raised his hand and gestured to her to go back home.

"The kite," he said.

"What's that?" she asked.

"Go," he murmured, raising the other hand.

"What are you doing standing up there like that, Santi?" she asked very softly.

"Go, just go," he repeated, although his words sounded weak and distant.

A claw ripping at his stomach made his lips curl up and he grimaced with pain.

"What's the matter? Don't you feel well?" she asked, taking a step forward.

Santiago stammered something but it was as if his mouth was full of sand. His eyes were filling with tears and there was nothing he could do about it. He felt a strain on his nape, a force that was pressing down on his neck and shoulders and crushing his back. His body was once again slow and heavy. The stench of the summer heat filled the air and made it hard for him to breathe. Soon he began to make out street noises and when the sudden sound of a jet blasted into the night, he shut his eyes and covered his ears. As he did so, he reeled backwards and he staggered a couple of steps along the wall.

"Santiago!" his wife screamed, but he had already regained his balance.

"What's wrong, mum?" he heard Roberto saying.

Santiago looked at his son. His hair was all dishevelled and he was only wearing the bottom part of his pyjamas.

"What's dad doing? Has he been drinking again?"

"Be quiet, Roberto," she said firmly, without raising her voice. "And don't move," she added. Then she turned to her husband and spoke to him imploringly:

"Why don't you get down now? It's starting to get cold..."

Santiago gritted his teeth. A tear was rolling down his right cheek. That was it. He'd lost his chance.

"Please get down," she insisted in a voice that was on the verge of breaking. "Do it for me. Come on, get down and let's go back to bed."

He shook his head several times without speaking. Then he sank his chin into his chest.

She stretched out her hand and walked towards him, very slowly, as if she was walking barefoot over a floor covered with broken glass.

Santiago was still, looking down, his

arms dangling by his side. When she reached him and took his hand it was like holding a cold, lifeless fish. She turned to her son and said:

"Can you come here now, Roberto?"

The boy nodded. He was a bit bewildered, as if he still hadn't quite woken from a dream. He took his father's other hand and between them they helped him down. Santiago let them do it, like an automaton.

"The kite," he muttered.

"What did he say?" Roberto whispered to his mother, who just shook her head.

"The kite," he repeated, while his son grasped him around the waist and placed one of his father's arms over his shoulders.

Just then, Roberto remembered the countless times his mother had got him out of bed in the middle of the night. His father had fallen asleep in the armchair in his study, with his head lolling forward before the blank screen of his computer, glass still in hand. The boy, still half asleep, would help his mother lift him and together they would drag him to the bedroom.